For my Big Sis
From Squirt

HarperCollins
PUBLISHERS

Balzer + Bray is an imprint of HarperCollins Publishers.
Little Penguin and the Lollipop. Copyright © 2017 by Tadgh Bentley. All rights reserved. Manufactured in China. No part of this book may be used or reproduced in any manner whatsoever without written permission except in the case of brief quotations embodied in critical articles and reviews. For information address HarperCollins Children's Books, a division of HarperCollins Publishers, 195 Broadway, New York, NY 10007.
www.harpercollinschildrens.com

ISBN 978-0-06-256078-0

All illustrations for this book were drawn using pen and ink and colored digitally.
Typography by Dana Fritts
17 18 19 20 21 SCP 10 9 8 7 6 5 4 3 2 1
❖ First Edition

Tadgh Bentley

Little Penguin and the Lollipop

BALZER + BRAY
An Imprint of HarperCollinsPublishers

Oh! Thank goodness you're here! I really need your help. . . .

It's my friend Kenneth. He's a little upset, and I think I know why.

You see, I ate
Kenneth's lollipop.

It looked ever so delicious.
I couldn't help myself.

How was I supposed
to know it belonged to
someone else?

I don't know if this has ever
happened to you, but let me
give you some advice:

never take

a

a lollipop from seagull

It makes them very grumpy.

I feel terrible about it.
So I tried to make it up to Kenneth.

I gave him a hug.

I told him how delicious his
Razzle-Dazzle Seaweed Lollipop was.

I even wrote him an "I'm sorry" card.

None of it worked.

But now you're here! I've got one more idea—and you are the perfect person to help.

Just do what I do. . . .

Make a funny face and repeat after me . . .

RAZZLE-DAZZLE LOLLIPOP!

Ready?

1-2-3...

Razzle-
Dazzle
Lollipop!

Well, that got his attention, but he's not smiling yet. Let's try again, even sillier.

Make a funny face, wave your flippers, and yell even louder.

Ready?

1-2-3...

Razzle-
Dazzle
Lollipop!

ARRGH!
Nothing is working!

Let's try once more. SUPER goofy this time. . . .

Make the funniest face you can,
wave those flippers in the air, jump up
and down, and REALLY shout.

Ready?

1-2-3...

Razzle—

Dazzle

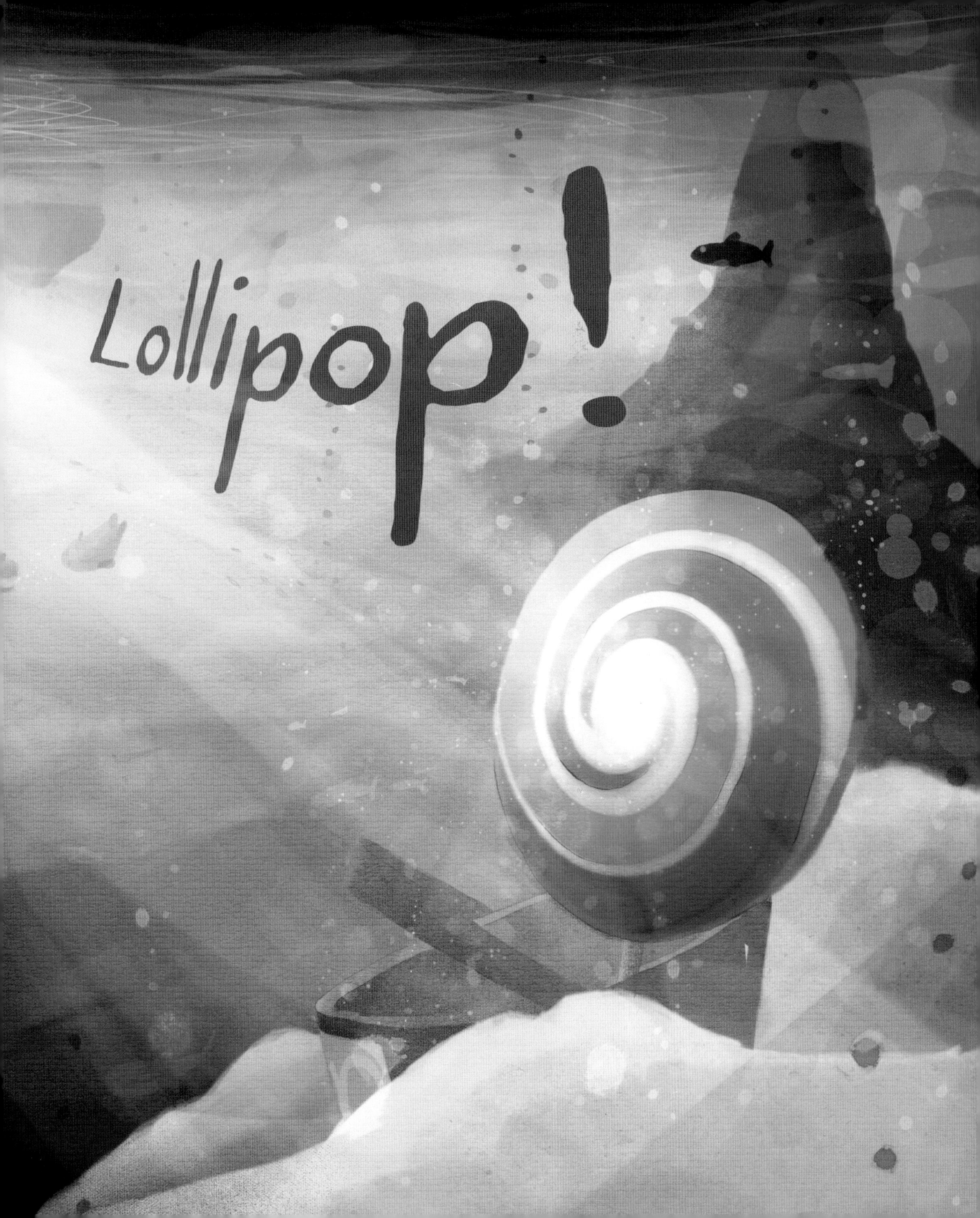
Lollipop!

A Razzle-
Dazzle
Seaweed
Lollipop,

just for you!

I'm glad you like it!

It looked ever so delicious.

It was just lying there,
waiting for me to pick it up.

But I'm sure that THIS lollipop
doesn't belong to anyone else. . . .